Jonathan and His Mommy

Jonathan and His Mommy

by Irene Smalls

Illustrated by Michael Hays

Little, Brown and Company

Boston   New York   Toronto   London

First Paperback Edition

Library of Congress Cataloging-in-Publication Data
Smalls, Irene.
    Jonathan and his mommy / by Irene Smalls; illustrated by
Michael Hays. — 1st ed.
    p.   cm.
    Summary: As a mother and son explore their neighborhood, they
try various ways of walking — from giant steps and reggae steps to
crisscross steps and backward steps.
    ISBN 0-316-79870-3 (hc)
    ISBN 0-316-79880-0 (pb)
    [1. Walking — Fiction. 2. City and town life — Fiction. 3. Mother
and child — Fiction.] I. Hays, Michael, 1956– ill. II. Title.
PZ7.S63915Jo 1992
[E] — dc20   91-31797

10 9 8 7 6 5 4 3

WOR

Published simultaneously in Canada by Little, Brown & Company
(Canada) Limited

Printed in the United States of America

I like to go walking and talking with my mom.

First we zigzag walk down the street;
It looks strange to the people we meet.

Then we take big giant steps, big giant steps,
And talk in loud giant voices,
And we say big things the way giants must talk:
"I say, did you see
That hu-mon-gous mammoth among us?"

After that we take itsy-bitsy baby steps,
Itsy-bitsy baby steps,
And talk in tiny baby voices
About baby things: itsy-bitsy spiders,
Tiny dreams, and small marshmallows.

Next we take bunny steps,
Hop-hop hop-hop-hop (hip-hop, too, sometimes),
As we wriggle our noses and wiggle our ears;
We look so funny that we end up in tears.

SLOW

CHILDREN
AT PLAY

8AM-4PM
MON-FRI

Tears that dry with the wind
As we take fast running steps, fast running steps,
Running our race.

You're the winner, I'm the misser,
I see on my mom's face.
Sometimes she can't keep up with my fast pace.

So I slow it down,
And we do slow-motion steps,
Sloow-moootion steps,
As we talk about molasses
And birthdays and how long they take.

And just before we're about to fall asleep . . .

We take a leap onto our toes
And do ballet steps, ballet steps,
Arms in the air, twirling round and round,
Till our feet touch the ground.

Then we do crazy crisscross steps,
Crazy crisscross steps.
Mommy steps and I step,
And our legs cross;
Mommy steps and I step,
And our legs crazycross.
The one who makes the last step
Is the boss of the crisscross.

After crossing a fast and our last crisscross,
We move on to reggae steps, reggae steps,
Hips swaying, feet step-step-sliding side to side,
Bodies moving to the beat of our hearts.

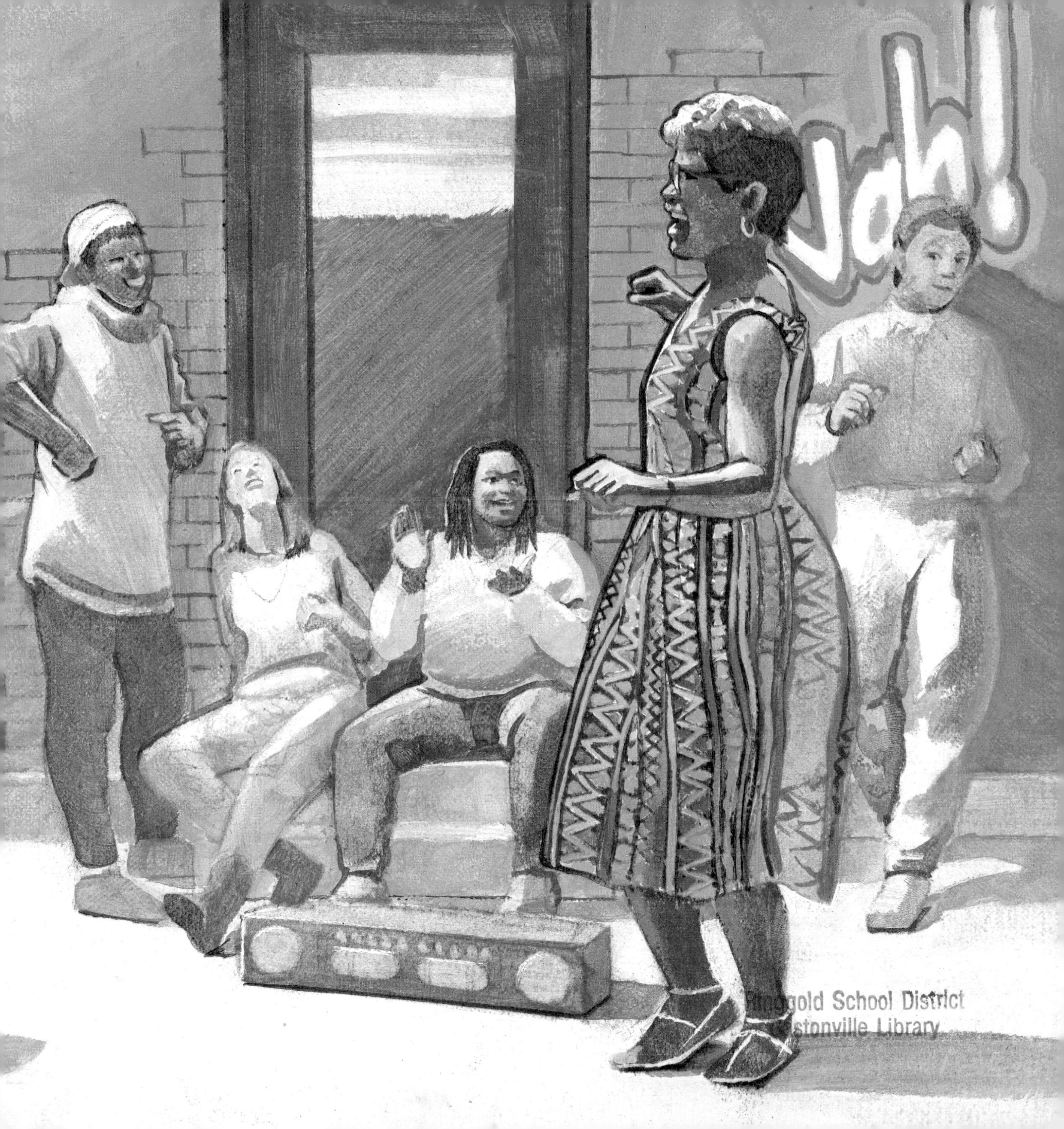

Then we take backward steps, backward steps,
And go to all the places we've been . . .

Which is good because
By that time we're tired . . .

And we take Jonathan-and-Mommy steps,
Jonathan-and-Mommy steps,
And walk our way home.